KITES & DRAGONS

STORIES OF CHINA, JAPAN AND BURMA
FOR 7–9 YEAR-OLDS

BY

MURIEL R. WRAY

AUTHOR OF

The Red Friendly Book, Along the Forest Path,
Talks on Chinese Disciples

ILLUSTRATIONS BY

ELIZABETH E. BEVAN

CONTENTS

TWO STORIES OF CHINA

TWO STORIES OF JAPAN

A STORY OF BURMA

THE TALE OF A KITE

EVERY boy in China was thinking about kites. The crisp autumn air told him that the kite flying season had come. In the courtyards of any houses where there were boys with time to play, clever fingers were making kites. First they built the framework of thin, thin strips of bamboo, then they cut brightly coloured tissue paper into shape, stretched it across the bamboo and stuck it in place. As they worked, the boys were turning the kites of their dreams into real shapes that would fly higher and higher as the wind carried them up to the clouds. The shops were full of kites too. Some were made to look like birds or butterflies or fishes or dragons or aeroplanes. Others were curious creatures unlike anything that ever lived.

Ming Kuei [1] was just seven and his mind was very full of kites. He had been to look at all the kite shops in the town but he had not bought a kite. This year he had made a kite of his very own. Now he meant to fly it *all by himself*.

[1] Pronounce Kway.

But first he must show Ming Zen, his sister, what he had made. He knew just where she would be. She always lay on her bamboo couch in her bedroom, for she could not walk and run like other girls. But though she could not use her legs, her fingers were never idle. She helped her mother to make clothes and cloth shoes for the family. Sometimes she drew flower patterns for the neighbours when they wanted to embroider pictures in silk. Ming Kuei was sure that no one could draw better pictures, sing more rhymes, nor tell more stories of adventures than this sister of his.

This afternoon Ming Zen was looking through the open window by her bed. The window opened into the courtyard and she was watching the door in the opposite wall that led to the street, watching for Ming Kuei to come back with the kite he had made. As she waited, thinking of kites, she sang a little rhyme to herself :

> " There were two little sisters went walking one day,
> Partly for exercise, partly for play,
> Their kites they took with them they wanted to fly
> Were a big centipede and a big butterfly.
> In a very few moments they floated up high,
> Like a dragon that seemed to be touching the sky."

Then the street door burst open and in rushed Ming Kuei, kite and all. What a fat little fellow he looked in his padded clothes ! Mother had made the long blue cotton gown that reached almost to his ankles. The short black jacket that he wore on top Ming Zen had made for him all by herself. His small round black satin cap with the red button on top stuck on his smooth round head. He held out his new treasure for Ming Zen to see as he ran across the courtyard and soon came tumbling through the door into her room.

"See what a beauty it is!" he said, all breathlessly.

And indeed it was. It was made of thin red tissue paper in the shape of a big fish, with blue scales and a large head of more colours than Ming Zen could count all in one look.

"It's lovely," said Ming Zen. "Please, may I hold it? What a splendid long tail it has."

"My fish will soon be touching the sky. I'm going out to fly it now," Ming Kuei announced.

Ming Zen looked out of the window again. The bamboo trees that grew on the other side of the wall were very still. "There isn't much wind. Do you think it will fly?"

"Of course it will. I'll whistle for the wind like the boatmen do," said Ming Kuei stoutly; "and I'm going to take a big ball of string to reach from here to the sky."

Ming Zen knew where string was to be found and told Ming Kuei where to look. "Good-bye," she called as he set out again, "and mind your big fish does not swim into the sky with you at the end of its tail!" But Ming Kuei wasn't really listening.

There were sounds from the kitchen of supper being prepared, and Ming Kuei thought he had better look to see how nearly ready it was. He was very careful not to catch his mother's eye. He wanted to go kite flying and she might call him to take the rice and wash it in the little canal by the roadside.

The very old woman who helped his mother in the kitchen was hobbling to the door to open it for the water coolie. Ming Kuei stood back but stayed to watch the man as he brought two heavy wooden buckets, brim full of water. The buckets were swinging from the two ends of the strong bamboo pole he balanced on his shoulder. "Ai-ay. Ai-*ah*. Ai-ay," sang the coolie as he came along the street. "Ai-ay. Ai-*ah*. Ai-ay," as he came across the courtyard and through the kitchen door. It seemed to help him to carry his load.

Then into the tall earthenware *kang* that stood in the kitchen went the water and scarcely a drop was wasted. Ming Kuei could only just see over the top of the *kang*, it was such a big jar, and yet it seemed to need filling many times. He always liked to be about when the water coolie came. When the coolie had gone, the old woman who helped sat down by the door again and went on sewing shoe soles ; mother went on making dumplings, and no one had time to take much notice of Ming Kuei. "There's plenty of time to go out," he said to himself.

In the guest room Ming Fu, Ming Kuei's elder brother, was reciting his lessons for the next day at school. He looked

and felt important in his new school uniform. He wore a short coat and long trousers, instead of a long gown like Ming Kuei, and brass characters, or letters, fastened into his high collar, told the name of his school. He was reciting his lesson in a very loud voice, swaying to and fro as he chanted. It did not sound as if Elder Brother would come out kite flying that day. Still carrying his kite very carefully, Ming Kuei slipped out through the door into the street. Only Ming Zen saw him cross the courtyard.

In the street there were many people and much noise.

All the coolies with loads to carry chanted as they trotted along. An old woman sitting on the ground weaving a big straw hat, made way for him to pass. " Eh, Ming Kuei, where are you taking that fine new kite ? " she asked.

" I'm going to make it fly," he said.

" But there isn't any wind," said the woman.

Ming Kuei looked at the bamboos that grew behind the houses and saw that they stood very still. But he nodded to the old woman and went on down the street.

Now someone was coming towards him, singing, and Ming Kuei knew the song of his old friend the cake man very well.

" Come buy my cakes, come buy my cakes,
They can cure the deaf and heal the lame,
And preserve the teeth of the ancient dame."

Sometimes Ming Kuei wondered if all that the song promised about the cakes could possibly be true. Ming Zen was lame and the old man's cakes had never made *her* any better. To-day Ming Kuei had no money to buy cakes.

" Where are you taking your kite ? " the old man asked him.

" I'm going to the country to make it fly."

" It's no use trying to-day. There isn't any wind," said the old cake man.

Ming Kuei looked at the bamboos behind the houses and they still stood very still. But he nodded to the cake man and went on.

On and on trudged Ming Kuei with his new kite, through the gates of the town and out into the country. The farm workers were coming from the fields, tired dusty farm workers, with wide straw hats that shaded their eyes and thick straw sandals to protect their feet.

A large buffalo, with flat back-curving horns and a long black snout, came ambling and swaying along the path towards Ming Kuei. A very little boy was sitting on its back holding on to its horns with his fat little hands. A small round tuft of hair stuck up from the baby's shaved head, and he gave a long and very solemn look

at Ming Kuei's kite. He looked as if he liked the kite, and he was much too little to say " But there isn't any wind to-day." Ming Kuei liked the baby and would have stopped to talk to him but the buffalo seemed to know it was in charge and just plodded on. Then came a jolly farmer's boy, just Ming Kuei's own age. He was riding a buffalo too.

" What a splendid kite," said the farmer's boy, looking from under his very big straw hat. " It is a pity there isn't any wind to-day."

Ming Kuei looked at the clouds, white clouds in a blue sky, and some of them seemed to be moving a little. So he nodded to the farmer's boy and went on, taking the path to the hills.

Soon he was climbing the uneven stone steps up the hillside, past the vegetable gardens, and through an orchard of peach trees. The farmers had made giant steps, terraces on the hillside, to hold the water for their thirsty rice plants. Ming Kuei wished that his legs were long enough to mount by that stairway, but that would need the giant's seven-league boots. So on he went, on his own short legs, up the uneven stone steps. He came to a level place on the hillside. "This should be a good kite-flying place," he thought. He remembered what the river boatmen did when they wanted more wind to fill their sails, and he turned to the east and whistled for the wind to come. Ming Zen sometimes sang :

> "Old Grandmother Wind has come from the east,
> She's ridden a donkey—a dear little beast."

But even the whistle and the rhyme together made very little difference. He held up the lovely new kite as high as his arm would reach and ran back, but it only fluttered to the ground. As he bent to pick it up he heard a voice speaking to him in strange foreign Chinese : "There isn't any wind here, but at the top of the hill there is a strong breeze blowing."

Ming Kuei looked up and was very much surprised to see a white-faced foreign lady and her little girl. The white lady had blue eyes and curly yellow hair that Ming Kuei thought ugly and most untidy. *His* mother's hair was quite black and very smooth, and she always wore it in a tidy coil at the back of her head. Ming Kuei was so busy looking at the foreigners he almost forgot to give the polite greeting and to say "Thank you" for the news about the breeze on the hill-top. He knew where the foreign people lived, he had seen them pass his house and go into the Way of Life Hospital. He had heard that the foreign man knew how to make sick people well. So he was not afraid, but showed them his fine new kite and said, "I'm going to fly it all by myself to-day."

Jennifer, the foreign girl, and her mother were coming

down the hill, so Ming Kuei had to go on all by himself right to the top. The steps were growing steeper and Ming Kuei went more slowly. He could see boys and girls gathering fuel for the evening fires, and stacking leaves and grasses and twigs in the big baskets they carried on their backs. How greedy the fires were ! Ming Kuei sang the song of the fire and the tune helped him up the hill, just as the coolies' songs seem to help them along.

> " Little red fire, burn slow, burn slow,
> You frighten me when you shoot up so,
> Making one mouthful of *kaoliang* stalks
> I gathered for you on my weary walks.

> " Little red fire, glow red, glow red,
> To warm the *k'ang* for my winter bed ;
> Please eat as little as ever you can,
> Fuel is so dear for a poor old man.

> " Little red fire, I beg your grace,
> Stay in your own little cosy place.
> Why dance to the roof like a scampering **mouse** ?
> Just heat the oven and spare the house."

The nearer he got to the top of the hill the more he could see of the town. He could see the mound of the city wall and the tiled gables of the gates. The evening sun was shining on the yellow glazed tiles of the temple roofs. Grey-robed priests stood by the doorway and Ming Kuei could see the people going in to worship. He knew that each carried a prayer written on a yellow paper scroll that the priests would burn for them. " Crackle crack, bang ! " Even high on the hillside he could hear the sound of the crackers that were let off as prayers were burnt, and puffs of smoke from the temple fireworks curled up in the still air, above the yellow temple roof. At last he reached the top of the hill. Now the trees were dancing, yes at last, here was the very wind for a new kite !

Quickly he uncoiled some of the string, took the precious fish in his hand, ran a little way with it and let it go. Then he ran back to pick up his ball of string. Up and up sailed the kite. How lovely it looked ! Higher and higher " swam " the fish in the clear evening air, and Ming Kuei was so proud of it. The town below looked so small now.

He wondered if his fish could still see the priests and the worshippers and the coolies and the cake man and the red tiled roof of his very own home. Perhaps the fish was trying to see beyond the clouds ? It was tugging now so hard that Ming Kuei's arms ached with trying to hold his end of the string. The kite tugged to go up higher and Ming Kuei tugged to hold it tight and then—snap went the string ! Ming Kuei sat down very suddenly and the kite, as if it was glad to be free, sailed away over the hills, over the terraces and the vegetable gardens, away towards the town.

Ming Kuei picked himself up feeling very sad indeed. His lovely kite was lost and there was nothing to be done but trudge home again, down all those stone steps, through the gates into the town, and home. With just a ball of string in his hand, feeling rather cold, very hungry and miserable, Ming Kuei turned down the hill. Now that he was not carrying a splendid kite no one stopped to tell him there was no wind to-day. He knew better!

Ming Kuei came into the courtyard very quietly this time. It was getting dark, and he hoped no one would notice him. But father was there stacking bamboo poles in a corner, ready for his workmen to-morrow.

"Ah, there you are," he said, "and where is that new kite?"

Ming Kuei hung his head. "I have lost it. The string broke on the hill-top and it has flown away."

Ming Fu, who was standing in the house doorway, laughed, but Ming Zen called from her room: "Never mind, Ming Kuei, save up your *cash* to buy paper and I will help you to make another kite."

Just then mother called them to supper and Ming Kuei remembered how very hungry he was. There was room for eight people to sit at the square table where the food was set. Mother brought chopsticks from the long narrow basket on the kitchen wall where they were kept during the day. A small bowl heaped high with steaming rice was set for each of them. In the middle of the table were the family bowls that everyone shared—one held pork dumplings; another fresh bamboo shoots with lots of thick, good-smelling gravy; another mixed vegetables—chopped carrots and turnips and peas that had grown in the hillside gardens; a fourth was filled with shrimps; and the fifth with dried fish and mushrooms. Everyone dipped into the family bowls for the things he liked best and added the good things to his own pile of rice. Ming Kuei held his own bowl quite close to his mouth and then shovelled the rice in with his chopsticks. He was much too busy now to talk, and the old woman had to fill his bowl three times before he stopped being hungry. But while he was eating he was wondering how soon or how long it would be before he had enough *cash* to buy paper for a new kite.

Ming Fu was just going to light the lantern that hung outside the door when they all heard a knock. " Who can be calling now ? " they wondered. Mother went to the kitchen to see if the water was boiling, for if visitors came they must be offered tea. Ming Kuei listened and heard a voice that had spoken to him before that day, the voice of the foreign lady with the yellow hair. He peeped round the door, and sure enough there she was, and Jennifer was with her. She had something big in her hand, but it was dark outside and he could not see what it was.

" Please come in," said Ming Kuei's mother, coming out of the kitchen.

" I have brought back this ; the wind blew it over into the hospital garden and it caught in a tree. Jennifer remembered where you lived. I am afraid the kite is a little broken."

And there was Ming Kuei's wonderful fish kite with a torn tail ! Ming Kuei's eyes shone with delight. " Oh thank you very, very much," he said, and then he ran to tell Ming Zen all about it.

" We are indeed unworthy that you should trouble yourself about my small son's kite," said Ming Kuei's mother. Then she made tea, and while the grown-up people sat and drank it, Jennifer and Ming Kuei talked to Ming Zen.

Father explained, " Ming Zen does not run or walk. We have prayed to many gods but the child is no better. Her fingers are clever and she can embroider and draw pictures, but what is the use of a girl who cannot walk ? "

" May I see her ? " Jennifer's mother asked. " Perhaps we might be able to help her to grow strong. One day will you bring her to the Way of Life Hospital ? "

When Jennifer's mother went to see Ming Zen she found her drawing pictures for Jennifer and Ming Kuei. She smiled

at them and said, " One day, Ming Zen, we hope you will come and let us see if we can teach those legs to walk and help you to grow strong."

That seemed rather like a dream to Ming Zen, but she did not forget. She heard the family saying good-bye to the visitors at the door. " Good-bye. Good-bye. Walk slowly," they called, and Jennifer's mother answered in the polite way, " Good-bye. We have been poor company. To-morrow we will look for Ming Fu and Ming Kuei when the boys fly kites from the hospital garden."

Then night came and darkness in all the town. Ming Kuei and Ming Fu slept on their bamboo beds, kept warm by wadded cotton quilts underneath and rolled round them. From the temple came the sound of the priests chanting, singing prayers to their gods, then came the sound of a temple drum and then the town was quiet, as all the people slept, except the night watchman who banged his bamboo as he marched through the sleepy town.

The next day the wind had come down from the hills and was making the bamboo trees among the houses dance and sway. Ming Kuei, his fish kite cleverly mended by Ming Zen and with a much stronger string, was waiting impatiently for his elder brother to come back from school. Were they not to fly kites together ?

" Remember to go and fly your kites in the hospital garden," Ming Zen pleaded.

When Ming Fu came home he would not promise, and as Ming Zen watched her brothers go with their kites she could only go on hoping they would bring back news of the Way of Life Hospital. At least they had turned in the right direction when they went through the gate.

Ming Fu did not say any more about the hospital, but they went on walking towards it. Soon they came to the gate, which stood wide open, and there was Jennifer standing outside, waiting for them. " I'm so glad you've come," she said, " and that your lovely fish kite will fly again. See what a fine breeze there is to-day."

Ming Fu and Ming Kuei looked through the round gateway into the garden. They saw a wide, open playing field and several boys and men with kites. Jennifer's father was with them and he had a kite too. How pretty it all looked, and this good brisk breeze was made for flying kites ! Gaily coloured kite birds and animals and butterflies had started to climb towards the clear sky and were tugging at their strings. Some of the boys were playing kite games together, trying to hook one another's kite to capture it.

"Come along," said Ming Fu, in a hurry now to join the fun. "My kite will win, I know." And he went through the gate and threw his kite bird up towards the sky. Jennifer and Ming Kuei flew the fish together, and with two people to hold it down to earth it decided not to fly away this time.

Before they went home Jennifer's father said, "Would you like to see inside the Way of Life Hospital?" And Ming Fu and Ming Kuei said, "Yes, please."

He took them into a long room full of sunshine, with beautiful pictures on the walls and rows of beds and cots covered with brightly coloured quilts. In the beds were children, who all seemed to be as full of smiles as the room was full of sunshine. "This is the children's ward," said Jennifer's father, "and we are hoping that your sister will come and stay here for a little while. Do you think she would like to come?"

Ming Kuei thought that she would, and when they went home they told her all about what they had seen.

.　　　.　　　.　　　.　　　.　　　.

Then one day father and Ming Fu carried Ming Zen to the Way of Life Hospital. Now she is getting stronger every day.

When Ming Kuei goes to see her she has many wonderful new stories to tell. "One day," she told him, "I may be able to walk like Jennifer and like you. Jennifer's father says the Lord Jesus sent him here to help us to grow well and strong. When I am better will you let me help you to fly a kite?" And Ming Kuei has promised that he will.

FIFTH DAY, FIFTH MONTH

HAVE you ever opened your eyes, before the sun was up, wondering WHY you had wakened so early, and WHY you felt excited, and WHAT was special about to-day ? That is just what happened to First Sister, when she woke up one June morning in her home in a village in China.

She knew that she felt hot, very hot indeed, and though she turned and twisted she couldn't find a cool place on her hard bed, although it was spread with a sheet of fine grass matting. Even her little hard oblong pillow felt hot. The dark room seemed full of noisy, buzzing mosquitoes, and one bold, wide-awake fellow sat on Elder Brother's shaved head and gave him a stab. Perhaps that was when *he* remembered, as he hit out at the " buzzer," that to-day was Fifth day of Fifth month ! Fifth day of Fifth month was always hot with midsummer heat, but there were other things about it that you wanted to remember. It was a day when you all wore new clothes, when your friends gave you pretty charms and scent sachets to dangle from the buttons on your shoulder, when you ate special food and, most exciting of all, it was boat-race day.

B

The more First Sister remembered the more wide awake she became. This year father was drummer for one of the boats, and all his crew were to be dressed in scarlet. Most exciting of all, Elder Brother had been chosen to hold the strings and waggle the great paper dragon's head, with which the scarlet boat was decorated. So his new coat was scarlet, too. When First Sister remembered all *that*, she didn't try to go to sleep again but jumped out of bed. This most exciting of days must be as long as ever wide-awake people could make it.

Elder Brother did not put on his new scarlet clothes directly he got up. An old pair of thin blue grass-cloth trousers were quite good enough to begin the day. He put up his hand to touch the twisted silver chain that father had fastened round his neck. "That will keep you safe from evil spirits and help to bring luck to our boat," father had said a long time ago. Yes, it was still there, and Elder Brother was glad. He was rather afraid of the spirits that might be wandering about on a festival day. He sat on the edge of his low bamboo bed, with his bare feet on the cool, smooth floor-boards.

Now it was getting light enough to see the shape of things in the room in which they slept, the rough mud walls and the dusty thatch of rice straw overhead. Without waking their father and mother, Elder Brother went through the living-room into the courtyard, and First Sister followed him. A row of giant sunflowers, nearly as tall as Elder Brother, grew in the shelter of the outer wall, but the flowers were still in bud. Father's wooden plough and buckets were stacked away in a corner. The mats of plaited straw that were so often spread on the ground, when rice or bright red pepper-pods or leaves from the tea bushes had to be dried, were rolled up and put away under the over-hanging thatch of the wall. The courtyard, usually so very full of rubbish and useful things, looked empty and seemed to be inviting people to play in it.

" Let's play dragon-boats," said First Sister, looking rather longingly at the bare space. " I'll fetch father's drum and gong and you could beat it."

" Phew, I'm too hot," gasped Elder Brother. " I'm going to the stream for a splash."

A heavy wooden door led from the courtyard to the street, and at night time it was fastened across by a strong bar. Elder Brother lifted the bar, opened the door and stepped outside. Their home was at the end of the twisty line of houses that made the village. The flat country beyond looked like a giant chess-board—bright, bright green squares of growing rice were divided by tiny straight canals and raised paths. The morning mist was rising slowly from the fields. It looked as if they were waking too, and saying good-bye to their dreams. Above the strands of dream-mist the two by the door could see bare red hill-tops, just touched by the rising sun.

" That's where the Water Dragon lives," said First Sister, pointing to the highest hill, the first one that had caught a sunbeam.

" I hope he will send luck to the scarlet boat," said Elder Brother. " See, the morning sun has given his mountain home a scarlet cloak." And so it had !

Not many fields away Elder Brother saw two of his friends already working one of the giant water wheels that turned to draw up water from the stream and send it into the little canals between the squares. As the boys trod on the steps of the wheel it creaked and squeaked in its bamboo joints but did its work right well and sent tiny waves of water coursing between the green squares to water the thirsty fields. The moving water had a cool sound, and Elder Brother was soon running towards his friends at the wheel. First Sister saw him splash the water over his face and arms, and hoped that it really did make him feel cooler.

Then mother called her in. Everybody seemed to be awake now and she was needed to help prepare rice for

the *chung-tsi*, the special food for Dragon Boat Day. All the picnickers beside the great rivers would have their packets of *chung-tsi* to eat, and of course the drummer and the dragon boy of the scarlet boat must have the best *chung-tsi* of all. First Sister knew that the Dragon Boat Festival was kept in honour of the hero, Chu Yuën, who had been drowned long ago in the River Yang-tse. Ever since then people had thrown rice in the river to feed his brave spirit. But they feared the rice was eaten by fish. So now the *chung-tsi* are always prepared, and the rice wrapped up to prevent the fish having a meal.

So mother and First Sister washed the rice. Then they took strips of palm leaves and made the rice into little three-cornered packages, and afterwards the packages were steamed. Elder Brother came back in time to help father fix a branch of sweet-smelling green leaves by the doorway, to help to keep the air clean and healthy on the festival day.

When they had eaten their breakfast rice and the bowls

and chopsticks had been washed and put away, it was time to put on their new clothes. First Sister was very glad that her long coat was made of cool, thin grass cloth. It was a lovely bright blue. It buttoned up under her chin and reached nearly down to her toes. Her brown eyes sparkled as she helped Elder Brother into his dazzling scarlet coat and thought of all the fun that was coming. Father wore a scarlet coat too. "You may carry this drum," he said, and Elder Brother took it and began to beat a tune.

"Tir-um-tee-tum. Tir-um-tee-tum. Trr-um. Trr-um.
That scarlet boat is sure to win. Row on. Row on,"

the drum seemed to be telling them as they went out into the street. First Sister would have liked to carry the gong and beat that. But father carried the gong himself and kept it very quiet and still.

The village street was full of people all in fine new clothes. The mothers and fathers, boys and girls and babies, grandmothers and grandfathers, aunts and uncles were hurrying towards the river. They followed single file along the narrow raised paths between the fields, calling to their friends in front of them and behind. Where many field paths met many voices joined in greeting.

It was getting more and more hot every minute. Elder Brother spied a man selling slices of cool-looking water melon;

father saw him too, and stopped to buy a slice for each of them. Elder Brother licked his lips. " I could eat a whole melon."

" Look," he said presently, " I can see the masts of the tall boats now."

First Sister was little, she couldn't see so far, but she was glad to know that they were near the river bank now. The laughing, happy crowds went on towards the little town by the river and through its narrow, twisting streets. " *Tir-um-tee-tum. Tir-um-tee-tum*," went Elder Brother's fingers on the drum, just because he felt happy.

At last even First Sister could see the masts of the boats. There seemed to be forests of masts. There were hundreds of boats swaying and bumping gently into each other as little wavelets came on the river. There were sailing boats with tall thin masts, barges, steamers, ·flat rafts, all close as close could be, lining the river on both sides. But there was a wide water pathway down the middle for the dragon boats.

" Come now," said father, pointing to the starting place. " The boatmen are getting into the dragon boats. We must go."

" *Tir - um - tee - tum. Tir - um - tee - tum*," said Elder Brother's drum once more, and the crowd made a way for the two in scarlet, who wished to reach their boat. Near the starting place the long boats were gathering. Each had a marvellous brightly coloured paper dragon's head fixed in front.

First Sister wriggled a little nearer the water's edge and then a boatman gave her a hand. " Stand on my poor raft," he said.

Mother and First Sister, telling him, most politely, that his was the best and the biggest raft that they had ever stepped upon, accepted his invitation gladly. His raft was almost in the front of the line of waiting boats, and standing on it even First Sister could see up the river pathway. Three boys in smart blue uniforms, with a red cross badge on their round black caps, shared the same raft. They greeted mother and First Sister most politely.

" Where do you come from and which is your school ? " mother asked them presently.

" We come from the Way of Life Hospital, and we are here to help, if anyone should fall into the river or be hurt in the crowd."

Mother thought it strange that anyone should trouble to help those who were not of their own family, but there was not time just then to ask them why.

" Look, look ! " squealed First Sister. " I can see the scarlet boat." Then she began to chant in a drum sort of voice, "The scarlet boat is sure to win ! Row on ! Row on ! "

" The yellow boat has the best crew. The yellow boat is sure to win. Row on ! Row on ! " teased one of the Red Cross boys.

" But *my* father is beating the drum and the gong on the scarlet boat, and Elder Brother guides the dragon's head," First Sister explained. And all the people on the raft understood that that *did* make all the difference.

The starting place was too far away for First Sister to see much more than the colours of the coats of the men in the dragon boats. One long boat was filled with men all dressed in green, another crew wore white, another orange colour and another brightest yellow. But the colour that First Sister could see best was scarlet !

At last all the boats seemed to be ready. The huge paper dragon heads of each boat were in a line across the water path. First Sister held her breath and waited. Even the noisy crowd was hushed for a minute. Bang went the starting gun, and away went the boats.   Fireworks were flashing and banging.   Everyone was shouting now.   But the largest and most exciting noise came from the boats themselves.   Twenty or thirty men sat in a double row in the long boat, each man digging the water furiously with his paddle.   At one end stood the steersman with a long oar

In the front a boy crouched behind the great dragon head, holding strings with which he made it move and sway and open and close its mighty paper jaws.   How like living dragons the boats looked !   Most important of all, in the middle of each boat stood a man with gong and drum who banged out the time for the crew.

First Sister watched the scarlet dragon head coming nearer and nearer, swinging from side to side with the swinging of the boat, just as if it were truly alive.   She could see Elder Brother plainly now as he crouched behind the dragon's head, pulling the strings that made the life-like side-to-side movement. She stood on tiptoe and leaned towards the coming boats. The men with the paddles were stirring the water into waves and foam. The waves danced across the river and made the rafts rock too. Now the scarlet boat was passing. It was well in front. First Sister was beating the drum time with her feet, the quick drum time that her father beat. She simply couldn't help it.

" Take care ! " called her mother's voice. " Take care, First Sister, you are too near the water ! "

But the warning came too late. There was a squeal and a big splash. First Sister had fallen into the river and knocked her head on the edge of the next boat as she fell. Almost before anyone on the raft had time to know what had happened there was another splash, and one of the boys from the Way of Life Hospital had jumped in after her. In a very few minutes his friends were helping them both back on to the raft, but it was a very wet, frightened First Sister, with a bumped head and a hurt leg. She could only just splutter " Who's won ? " But nobody could tell her.

Mother was afraid, too, and kneeling on the raft, knocking her head on the boards, was praying to all the gods she knew and begging them to hear and save First Sister. One of the boys put his hand on her shoulder. " Don't be afraid. See, First Sister is quite safe, but her leg has been hurt. Will you let us take her to the Way of Life Hospital ? In a day or two she will be quite well again."

Although mother was still very frightened, she remembered that these boys from the hospital had come to the race to be ready to help hurt people, and though she did not understand why they had come, she was glad they were there. At last mother said, " We will go with you."

The people on the raft helped mother and the hospital

boys to carry First Sister across the boats and back to the bank. After that it was not long before they reached the round gateway that led to the hospital garden. A smiling Chinese nurse, in a white uniform with a red cross on her sleeve, came to greet them. " You will like to stay with First Sister while we bandage her leg," she said, and of course mother stayed.

But she and First Sister were both too shy to say anything. (They would not have said that they were " shy," but that the skin of their faces was thin !) They just sat and looked and looked. Everything seemed strange. The rooms were so large and so full of light and colour. The walls were hung with pictures of Jesus and His friends. Even the floors shone with much polish. Nurses in uniform and the getting-better people, who walked past the window, all looked happy. First Sister wished she could talk to some of them and hear what happened to people who stayed in the Way of Life Hospital. Then the door opened, and a girl not much older than she was came in, bringing a clean, dry coat.

" This is Ming Zen," said the nurse, " and here is a coat for you to wear, while we wash and dry the one that went into the river with you." Then she turned to Ming Zen. " We would like First Sister to stay with us for a day or two, until she is quite better. Ming Zen has learnt how to walk since she came to us, haven't you ? " And smiling at them the nurse left Ming Zen to tell them all about it, as if she knew what First Sister had been wishing.

Mother and Ming Zen each shook hands with themselves, bowing to each other and said, " *Nitzi how ba.* How do you do ? " First Sister could not stand so she just bowed and shook her hands together as she sat propped up in the chair.

Then mother asked Ming Zen, " Do you live here ? "

" Not always. My home is in the town," Ming Zen answered. " My father and brother carried me when I first came, because never in all my life had I walked anywhere."

" But you can walk now, and I can't," said First Sister, looking rather sadly at her bandaged leg.

" Why yes, I can now,' said Ming Zen, " and I can run a little, too. The doctor says I shall be strong enough to help him to fly a kite when the cold weather comes." And she laughed because she was so happy.

" You never walked until you came here and now you talk of flying kites ! How did it all happen ? " mother asked. It all sounded almost too wonderful to be true.

" They put me in a bed in a room full of sunshine. Every day the nurse came and rubbed my legs with lotions. Then one day I could kick a little, and move my toes. Soon they let me try to stand, and slowly my legs learned to walk. In two more weeks I am to go home again, and this time my father and brother will not carry me. I shall walk all by myself."

First Sister had only just begun to ask some of the questions she wanted to ask when the nurse came back.

" Isn't it your turn to tell the story in the ward to-night, Ming Zen ? What is it about this time ? "

" It is the one about the Lord Jesus and His boatmen friends."

" Would you like to come in and hear it ? " the nurse asked mother and First Sister.

It sounded a good story, and into the big sunny room they went, and watched and listened.

First came music and singing that they did not understand. Then the nurse spoke to the God that the Way of Life Hospital people worship, and then everybody listened while Ming Zen told the story about the Lord Jesus and His friends in the boat.

When story time was finished and First Sister looked round, she said, " May I stay with Ming Zen until my leg is well ? " She wasn't a bit frightened now, and her mother said she might stay until father and Elder Brother could come to carry her home.

Ming Zen walked to the gate with mother and said, " Good-bye. Go slowly, and come soon to see First Sister."

But mother did not " go slowly," she hurried through the holiday crowds. She wanted to find father and Elder Brother and tell them of her adventures.

The next day mother, father and Elder Brother all came to the Way of Life Hospital to find First Sister. They found her sitting up in a little bed that had a scarlet cover over it and a white cross in the centre. Ming Zen was sitting beside her and had just finished drawing her a beautiful picture of a dragon boat, men with paddles, a very fierce dragon head at the front and a man in the middle beating a drum and banging a gong.

" Now let's give them coloured coats," Ming Zen was saying.

There, sure enough, was a paint box with rows and rows of beautiful colours.

" This is the boat that won the race. What colour shall we paint it ? " asked Ming Zen.

" Why, scarlet, of course ! " said Elder Brother.

" Oh, I *knew* you would win," said First Sister. " I'm so glad."

HONOURABLE MISS JEWEL

PICNICS are always fun, and when the sky is clear and blue
and the rain clouds very far away, then what could be
jollier than to pack a hamper with cakes and sweets and
fruit and go away to country places. If that is what you
think, then Honourable Miss Jewel agrees with you !

In cherry blossom time the corner of Japan that is her
home is a corner of fairyland. Here comes O Tama San
("Honourable Miss Jewel" is the English way of saying
her name) running down the steep cobbled path that leads
from her home to the high road. Her little thatched house
is perched on the mountain-side, and no wonder the path is
steep. O Tama San's brown eyes are dancing and there is
the tiniest pink flush in her pale oval face, but her straight
black fringe and her straight bobbed hair is as tidy and
shiny and smooth as can be. She is wearing her best
kimono of all, she chose the large gay-patterned stuff
herself. Her bright silk sash is folded so neatly, it looks

as if it grew just like that. Coming down the pathway behind her, very slowly and carefully, is O Baa San, the Honourable Grandmother. She is such a gentle little old lady, with straight white hair and a face covered with smile wrinkles. O Tama San does not forget to wait, now and then, to help O Baa San over the roughest parts of the cobbled path. Then comes father, wearing a straw hat and a dark cotton suit, made western way. Last of all mother comes, with baby brother. He is much too little to walk and so he has a snug nest in the back of his mother's coat, and his small dark head bobs up and down between her shoulders as she walks. Everyone is carrying a little box with picnic food in it. O Tama San knows just what is inside hers—delicious little rolls of rice with chopped-up fish and pickles inside, wrapped in black seaweed !

The road below Miss Jewel's house runs up a narrow valley and a hurrying, tumbling stream runs down beside the road. High on the mountain-sides she can see dark pine trees, and on the lower slopes bamboos that look like green feathers, light and always dancing with the breeze. But O Tama San loves the cherry trees best of all. They are everywhere, peeping between the wooden houses, sometimes standing close to a dark pine tree ; sometimes near the bamboo trees ; sometimes standing facing each other in long straight avenues ; and sometimes in orchards of their own, all laden with shell-pink blossom. So all the village is picknicking to-day. Even the workers at the silk factory, whose slender chimney towers above the clump of trees by the stream, have a holiday and can leave the noise and steam and heat of their work to enjoy blue sky and cherry blossom. O Tama San is soon dancing along with the rest of the happy, gaily-dressed crowd, bound for the cherry orchard.

At last they have come into the cherry orchard. It certainly is blossom time. Under the wide branches of a cherry tree O Tama San's mother and grandmother spread the meal. Baby brother sits on the ground and tries to catch the pearly petals as they fall, but O Tama San can catch many more than his tiny hands will hold, and he

laughs as she fills his lap. While the two children are playing the three grown-ups talk quietly, and sometimes their faces are sad.

" If we have no money we can buy no seeds for next year. What *can* we do ? We must have seeds for the fields." It is O Tama San's father who is speaking. " I have decided I can get work in the town for a time. O Tama San is big enough to be useful at home now."

That night her mother told her that father was going to the town to earn money to buy seeds for the fields.

"He may not be away very long!" she said, "but there will be lots of work for all of us and no time for picnics now, till he comes back."

And O Tama San remembered that her father had said she was "big enough to be useful now," so she stood up as straight and tall as she could and promised to help, and not mind about picnics.

. . . .

The weeks went by, the pink petals fell from the cherry trees and the tall iris flowers showed themselves in the gardens and stood close together beside the river in the valley. But O Tama San had little time to look at them. In their thatched house on the mountain grandmother, mother and O Tama San were the busiest people in all their village. Tama San was sure of that. All the days were very much alike except that the big family of silk-worms, that lived in one of the rooms of their house, grew hungrier and hungrier.

To-morrow would be the night of the Moon festival, a night for stories and for staying up late to watch the silver Lady of the Sky and offer gifts to her. O Tama San looked forward all the year to the Moon Lady's feast, but she remembered what her mother had said, and indeed there was no time for feasts. So she tried to forget and hoped that father would very soon come back. Perhaps another year there would be time. . . .

It was still dark in the little house when mother called O Tama San next morning. "It is time to be up and about, little daughter," she said.

Before she was quite awake a sleepy Miss Jewel got up from her cosy bed between the two soft quilts on the floor and bowed her head low to the ground as she said, "Good morning, Honourable Mother." Her hair looked as smooth and tidy as it had been the night before, for while she slept her neck had been resting on its wooden " pillow."

" Please may I open the screens this morning ? " she begged. She wanted to see what the sky was like on the morning of Lady Moon's day. " I'll be ever so careful and not put my fingers through one."

" Why, of course you may," said her mother, " but don't touch the big wooden shutters. O Baa San will help me to open those."

Sliding screens made walls between the sleeping room and the veranda of Miss Jewel's house. These were made of thick paper, stretched over a framework of wood. It was ever so easy to poke a finger through and make an ugly hole in the wall, and holes had to be mended !

This morning O Tama San pushed the screens gently, gently along the grooves, without touching the paper once. Mother and O Baa San were pulling up the wooden bolts and sliding the heavy shutters that made the outside wall of the veranda. The wooden " walls " fitted into a long box, and there they stayed all day.

When screens and shutters were open the cool sweet morning breeze came blowing through the little house, lifting the petals of the lovely yellow iris flowers that stood in a vase on the floor. O Tama San was sure they brought a morning greeting from the tall sister irises, yellow and purple and white, that were bowing towards them from the garden. The sky was clear and one star still sparkled. " Moon Lady, your day is fine," whispered O Tama San as she began to dress.

Mother, with baby brother on her back, took a tiny earthenware stove out of the kitchen into the yard, and soon the sweet scent of newly lit pine cones came into the house. O Tama San watched for a moment as mother blew the flames and the glow of the fire made her face rosy, like the sunrise

o

clouds across the valley. Then O Baa San called, and O Tama San bowed, " Good morning, Honourable Grandmother."

Water was wanted for tea making and for boiling the breakfast rice, and had to be drawn from a well in the yard.

" Come now, bring your water pot and help me to get the water."

O Tama San crossed the veranda and slipped her bare feet into the straw sandals that she had left outside in the porch. It would have been *very* bad manners to wear any shoes indoors. Honourable Miss Jewel's feet were small and the sandals big, and they flap, flopped as she hurried across the yard. How deep and cool and clear the water looked in the well !

" See, O Baa San, the pink clouds, like blossoms, are floating in the well."

O Baa San smiled. " That was nearly a poem, little granddaughter. The morning clouds will not stay in the sky, but you can keep that thought in your mind all through the day."

O Baa San and O Tama San went slowly across the yard, for the full water-pots were heavy. When father was at home he always helped to draw the water. Sandals off, they went into the kitchen, and O Baa San emptied their jars into an iron kettle that swung on a chain from the roof. It hung just over a square hearth sunk into the cement of the kitchen floor. This morning the white ash on the hearth looked cold and dead.

" Do you want straw to wake the fire again ? " O Tama San asked.

" No," said her grandmother, sitting on her heels by the hearth and stirring the fire with a little stick. " See, it has a warm heart still."

Sure enough, under the ashes was a warm red glow of charcoal, and O Baa San knew just how to waken it. Soon all the fire was glowing.

" Our kettle will soon be singing now," she said.

While mother cooked the breakfast O Tama San tidied the bed quilts. " One, two three," she counted, as she folded each quilt. They had to be folded in three to fit the deep cupboards with sliding doors where they lived in the daytime. All the floor of the room was covered with soft white mats woven from grasses, and O Tama San gave these their morning sweep.

By this time a good smell of breakfast was coming in from the kitchen and the yard. The wooden lid of the big rice pot was beginning to dance. O Baa San and mother lifted it together and hung a pot of bean soup in its place. O Tama San brought three square tables just twelve inches high, and set them on the floor. Then she brought three cushions and set them by the little breakfast tables. From a chest in the kitchen she fetched three bowls for the rice, three pairs of chopsticks, and three tiny teacup bowls. And a very good breakfast it was—hot rice, steaming bean soup, and clear tea without milk or sugar. When breakfast was over, bowls and chopsticks washed and put away, and the tiny tables and cushions stored in their cupboard home, the room was quite bare again except for the jar of iris flowers. And all the while, whenever O Tama San's tongue was still and baby brother was not crying for his breakfast, you could hear the rustle, rustle of the hungry silkworms, eating their meal that went on without stopping night and day.

" Will those honourable little gentlemen ever stop eating ? " O Tama San sighed, as she set to work to cut fresh mulberry leaves for the silkworms' next meal. One whole room in the house belonged to the hungry creatures. They lived on bamboo trays stacked on shelves, and at this time of the year everybody was busy feeding them. No wonder O Tama San had no time to play, no time to think about the

Lady Moon's feast, no time to walk in the garden among
the tall iris flowers. The trays had to be cleaned, and cleared
of all the rubbish, for " the honourable little gentlemen " are
most particular. Then O Tama San and her grandmother
went down the cobbled path, across the road and over the
dancing, never-tired river, up the hillside to the terraces
where the mulberry canes grew. They had no time to talk
to each other as they bent down to cut the canes. Some of
the stalks were nearly twice as tall as O Baa San herself,
but somehow she managed to balance a bundle on her
shoulders. O Tama San had her load too. Then home
they went, the long canes swaying as they walked with heads
bent under the burden, down from the terraces, across the
bridge, over the road and up the steep cobbled path that
led to home.

But still the silkworms were not satisfied. " More
please, more please, more please," they seemed to say as
they nibbled, nibbled, nibbled in their trays. Back went

O Tama San and her grandmother for another load, while mother, with baby brother on her back, cut up the fresh leaves. O Tama San's legs ached, and so did her back, but she was getting ready to trudge down the path and across the valley for the third time when her mother called her : " O Baa San will go alone this time. Would you like to make the round rice dumplings for Lady Moon's table ? "

O Tama San danced and clapped her hands. " Oh, may I really, all by myself ? I'll make them just as round as Lady Moon's own face."

So there *was* going to be time to keep the festival in honour of Lady Moon. O Tama San kept a little thought hidden in her mind. Surely Lady Moon, who sailed so high and saw so much of the world, must be able to do anything she pleased. Surely she would help to make father rich enough to come back very soon. Nobody in that little house in the mountains had ever heard about a loving Heavenly Father who watches over His children and understands when they are tired or afraid.

.   .   .   .   .

At last evening came and O Tama San was singing to baby brother. It was more than time he was in dreamland. She was sitting on the floor, and as she sang she rocked herself to and fro.

" Sleep, baby, sleep !
O where has thy nurse gone ?
She went away,
Far, far away
To thy grandmother's home.
She went away
Across the hills.
Soon she will bring to thee
Fish and red rice,
Fish and red rice
From thy grandmother's home."

O Tama San sang that because it was the best lullaby she could remember and the one with the sleepiest tune, but the only nurses baby brother knew were grandmother, mother and O Tama San, and it was father who was across the hills, far far away.

"Listen, Honourable Mr Baby, do you hear that?" From the house came the sound of a rustling and a rustling, like little raindrops falling on dry leaves. But no rain was falling. It was the noise of those hungry silkworms nibbling

their meal of mulberry leaves. "Listen and hear how hungry they are. That is good, little brother. The more they eat the fatter they grow. The more they grow the more golden silk they will spin for us. The more silk the more *sen*, and the more *sen* the sooner father will be able to come home."

But baby brother was too sleepy now to hear all that. Then mother came out in the porch, and O Tama San stood up to greet her. "See, I will take the little one now. Fetch your grandmother's cushion into the porch and see that the Moon table is all set. Look, the Lady Moon will soon be peeping in to see her gifts."

O Tama San turned to look through the open porch, and she gave a little gasp of joy. The round golden moon was shining her way through the grey mists and beginning to make all the June night beautiful with her light. O Tama San knelt on her mat and bowed to her.

" Good evening, most honourable Lady Moon. We are glad to see you. Look what is ready for you ! "

And if the Lady Moon *was* looking she could see a table spread with everything round that O Tama San and her mother could find to place there—round fruits, round vegetables and, in the centre, a plate of the roundest rice dumplings. Because O Tama San had made those dumplings all by herself she was sure that the Lady Moon would like them best of all the things she saw.

Moon nights were story nights, and so O Tama San was allowed to stay up long past her usual bedtime.

" One August evening long ago," grandmother began, " the Lady Moon was preparing for her journey across the sky. As she arranged her fluffy collar she said to herself, ' I've nothing to do but smile and look happy. It doesn't seem much, and really it is never very difficult. To-night, of all nights, it will be easy, for it is the Honourable Fifteenth when the Earth people have prepared a special welcome for me.' So, smiling with the happy thoughts of what she would see, she set out on her journey. Sure enough, in every porch of every house, from the richest to the poorest, tables were set outside or in the open porches, with round gifts to praise her perfect circle of light—rice dumplings, peas, chestnuts, round potatoes, round vases holding blossoms of her own moon flower—and songs of praise and welcome filled the air. Do you wonder she found it easy to smile that lovely night ?

" But Mistress Rain, who lived in the sky not far away,

was jealous. ' It isn't fair. They never make a fuss of me like that,' she said, and gave her skirts an angry little shake. Although it was only a little shake, all the umbrellas tied to her skirts flew open and some of the raindrops, with which they were always full, went scattering down to earth and made the people look up in surprise. Just as she began to shut the umbrellas again, the Wind god came grumbling by holding his bag of breezes. ' Good evening,' said Mistress Rain, ' you look as if you would like some fun to-night. How would it be to upset those tables the Earth people have set out for Lady Moon and send all the round things rolling ? ' ' Ho, ho,' roared the Wind god, and he rocked so much he loosed the ends of his bag of breezes. ' That would teach them that there *are* other people who live in the sky, as well as that smiling Lady. Come along. Let us show them.' So they slipped behind the mountains to come out on the other side and give the world a surprise.

" Lady Moon saw them go and, sad and disappointed, she went behind a curtain, all her pleasure spoiled. Then out came Mistress Rain and the Wind god from the other side of the mountains. Mistress Rain opened all her umbrellas and the Wind god threw every breeze out of his bag to hurry the raindrops. Swishing and roaring came wind and rain, but the Earth people were ready. Every shutter was safely closed and the lovely round Moon gifts were tucked away in the houses. So home they had to go, Mistress Rain weeping and the Wind god grumbling noisily.

" When they had gone, Lady Moon looked through her curtain. ' They have spoilt our Honourable Fifteenth this time and there will be no more Moon parties to-night. All the Earth people must be fast asleep, but I may as well go on shining, even if no one sees me.' So out she came again to go on her shining way.

" But the Earth people were *not* asleep. They opened their houses again and set the tables in their places. ' The Lady of the Sky is more beautiful than ever, after the storm,' they said, and the songs of praise they sang to her that night were the sweetest she had ever heard."

O Tama San sighed a deep sigh when grandmother finished. " I'm glad the Earth people did not go to sleep after the storm, and see now, O Baa San, how the Lady Moon is smiling. Do you think she likes the round rice dumplings that I made ? "

" Why surely, O Tama San, and now you must watch her in your dreams. It is time *this* Earth person went to sleep."

Mother was still busy with baby brother, so O Baa San opened the cupboard where the bed quilts were stored and took out the two that belonged to O Tama San. Then she slid the wooden shutters across the open porch and closed the screens. There was not a chink through which the Lady Moon could peep at O Tama San, asleep between two padded quilts, her neck resting on a little wooden pillow. O Tama San was dreaming, dreaming that the Wind god was trying to lead her father away to the other side of the mountains, but that the Lady Moon had shown him the way home instead. And all night long the " honourable little gentlemen " in the bamboo trays went on nibbling with a sound like raindrops rustling the dry leaves.

Away in the city somebody *was* taking care of O Tama San's father, but perhaps Lady Moon did not have much to do with it. What do you think ? And anyway, that is another story.

"LET'S LOOK FOR A FOREIGNER!"

TARO was feeling very important. A neighbour had called in to ask his father's help and father had said, "You can look after the shop for me till I come back. I shall not be away long." Taro was nine years old and this was the very first time he had been shopman, all by himself.

The front of the shop was open to the street. Summer and winter father slid the shutters back, so that the people passing along the street could see all the beautiful things he had for sale. Taro could see the people, too, as he sat on the floor at the back of the room. Soon two ladies stopped.

"Oh, do look at these! Why, here is a little carved lady just like our honourable mother. We must buy it for her."

Taro jumped up quickly and bowed as politely as father always did. The ladies smiled and soon went their way with the little carved wooden lady. Taro was proud of himself. He was a real shopkeeper now.

It was winter time and there was snow in the street. Very cold air was blowing in through the open front of the house. Taro could see snow on the tiled roofs of the houses opposite, snow tufts on the tips of the upturned corners, snow on the trees that peeped above the houses of the little Japanese street of shops. Inside Taro's shop shelves rose, one behind the other, like steps, from the pavement edge, and on every shelf were little wooden people that Taro's father had carved. Taro was sure no one could carve wooden people better than his father, and he meant to be a wood carver too.

When the customers had gone Taro sat on the floor again as close to the fire as he could get. The fireplace was a stone-lined bowl a few inches deep, sunk into the middle of the floor. A shovelful of bright glowing charcoal was put into the bowl and a high wooden frame stood over it. Over the top of the wooden frame a quilt was spread, and all the people who wanted to keep warm sat round the fire with the quilt over their knees. Taro had the fire and the quilt all to himself, but, of course, he had to keep his hands out in the cold while he worked. Once his knife slipped in his cold fingers and he almost cut himself, so he blew on his hands to warm them up and set to work again.

He was so hard at work he did not see his friend Haru standing in the street watching him. Haru was dressed in school uniform, exactly like Taro's. He had short trousers and a coat with a tight collar that buttoned at the neck. The uniform was made of speckly blue cloth. Both boys had shining brass buttons and Haru's cheeky, honey-coloured face was shaded by the peak of his school cap, but anyone could see his merry smile. Anyone, that is except

his friend Taro, who wasn't looking this time. Suddenly
Haru snatched one of the little carved wooden figures that
Taro's father had made, and, with a big scuffle of feet,
pretended to run away with it. Taro jumped up then,
ready to shout and run after him. Then he saw Haru and
knew that the "thief" was only pretending. Haru slipped
his feet out of the wooden clogs he was wearing and came
and sat by Taro, drawing the quilt over his knees too.

"What are you making?" he asked.

Taro sighed. "It *won't* come right. I've tried and
tried and his face isn't a bit the right shape. I think it is
his nose that is most wrong." He held up his carving for
Haru to see. "I wanted to make it for my honourable
father. It was to be my New Year gift to him. He has
made wooden figures of so many people, but he has never
made one like this."

Haru did not want to be rude but he really couldn't
see just what sort of a man Taro *was* trying to carve. "No,"
he said, putting his head on one side to get a better view,
"I don't think he has any like that in the shop."

The little wooden figures that Taro's father sold to the
people who passed along the street were all carved from
bits of birch wood. His clever fingers made tiny models of
the people who walked in the little street of shops and other
people from the country too. Here was a mountain climber
and here an old bent pilgrim dressed in a white robe and
carrying a pilgrim staff. Here were little country women
with backs bent by the heavy load of swaying mulberry
canes that they carried, and farmers in straw snow-shoes
and wide-brimmed hats. Here were dainty little ladies in
kimonos, carrying the tiniest umbrellas. And here were
jolly schoolboys with their bags of books, wearing uniform
and looking just like Taro and Haru.

" You see," said Taro, explaining, " all these that my father has carved are Japanese people, and I'm going to carve a foreign man, just for a surprise."

" Oh yes," said Haru, " so you are. Make him like the big one we saw at the pictures yesterday. He looked like this." And Haru jumped up and began strutting up and down, trying to look inches and inches taller than he really was.

But Taro was looking at his carving again. " It is the nose that is all wrong. I can't remember what those funny foreign noses are really like. Can you ? "

" I know," said Haru, who never could sit still for long, " let's go and look for a foreigner."

That seemed a good idea. So as soon as father came back Taro found his cap with a peak and, when the boys were just outside the shop, they both put on their wet-weather wooden clogs. Pathways had been cut through the snow down by the shops and across the streets, but how slippery they were ! Haru slid a little slide.

There was ever so much to watch in the street. The sky overhead was clear and the air full of sparkle. Some boys were playing marbles on a clear patch where the snow had been swept away. One boy had a baby brother tucked safely in the back of his coat, and he was playing and looking after the baby, all at the same time. Another group of boys were running races across the snow on stilts.

" They couldn't look after the baby and run on ' heron-legs,' could they ? " said Haru, as two of the stilt boys tumbled over each other and rolled laughing in the snow.

Three schoolboys, with painted kites under their arms, called to Taro and Haru : " Fetch your kites and come with us."

But Haru called : "We're busy. We'll come to-morrow."

People who are looking for foreigners have no time for flying kites !

The streets were very, very full of people and very full of decorations too. " In three more days it will be New Year holiday," said Taro, giving a little jump for joy. But he had forgotten how slippery the path was and had to clutch Haru to save himself from falling.

All the shops were getting ready for the New Year. Taro had helped his father to dig holes and plant two straight little pine trees one on each side of their door. " That is father pine on the left and mother pine on the right," they said. All the other shopkeepers had planted pine trees too. Some people had planted tall bamboo stems, and their green leaves danced in the wind above the low-tiled roofs. Ropes of plaited rice straw, hung with all kinds of strange and wonderful things, stretched from tree to tree. Taro and Haru knew what all the things meant, and as they bobbed under strings of oranges and cooked scarlet lobsters, lucky bags and strips of zigzag paper, they knew the people who had put them there were saying : " May all you people who shop in this street be wealthy and wise and live to be old."

And the shops were full of such exciting things, all waiting to be bought and taken home as New Year presents for mothers and fathers and brothers and sisters. Haru just *had* to stop once to spend some money he had in his pocket. It was a sweet shop that did it ! He and Taro went on their way, when Haru's money was spent, munching candy balls made of puffed rice and black sugar. They *did* taste good !

" Look," said Taro, as they passed by a shop that was full of books and pictures, " there is Mr Oguchi, the bookshop man. He knows lots of stories, wonderful stories that no one else in our street had heard before he came."

Mr Oguchi smiled at Taro and Haru and they bowed to greet him. He looked so friendly Taro and Haru wanted to stop and talk. Perhaps he would have time to tell them a story.

" Where are O Taro San and his honourable friend going now ? " he asked.

" We are looking for a foreigner," Taro explained.

" And what are you going to do with him when you have found him ? " asked the bookshop man.

" See what shape his nose is," said Haru with a grin. " Taru wants to look so that he can carve a foreign man in wood."

" What a pity you didn't come this way five minutes sooner. My foreign friend was here and you could have looked at him. His home is that way." Mr Oguchi pointed towards the big main road. " If you go quickly you may find him."

Taro and Haru bowed polite thanks. After all, they would not ask Mr Oguchi for a story just now. Then they ran up the little street towards the big main road. They were in a hurry and all the other people seemed to move

so slowly. The mothers, with their babies on their backs, stood outside the shops talking.

"Have you seen the foreign man?" the boys asked them.

"Why, yes, he has just gone by. Go quickly and you will find him."

That was what all the people answered when they asked them. So Taro and Haru went as quickly as they could through the crowds, and at last they came to the main road.

Electric trams and motorcars made the wide busy road difficult to cross. The rickshaw men were busy too, pulling with their chairs on wheels, running so quickly with their passengers. Some had trains to catch, some had shops to visit, some were hurrying to be home for tea. How slippery the road was! Taro wondered how the rickshaw men could run so fast without falling.

"Look!" shouted Haru suddenly, pointing across the road. "There he is. I can see his head above the crowd. Come along."

Haru turned to give his friend a tug forward, and they

both bumped into a country man who was hurrying towards the station. Because it was slippery they all three fell down with a crash. The man's bundles were scattered in all directions, and Haru's sharp eyes saw a little bag of what looked like money topple out of the man's pocket and go skidding along the slippery ground, far out of his reach. Haru dived almost under the wheels of a passing

rickshaw and rescued the money bag. When he came back Taro was up, and the man was sitting on the ground rubbing his knee. How glad he was when Haru gave him his money !

"Where are you going ? Can we help you ? " Taro asked.

"I was going to my home in the country, but I have missed the train and there is not another until to-morrow," said the man, trying to stand up. Taro and Haru helped him. He could stand, but when he tried to walk his knee hurt very badly.

D

The two friends looked at each other. A little crowd was gathering and asking what had happened. A rickshaw man with an empty chair stood by the path watching.

" We could go to Mr Oguchi," said Taro. " He always knows what to do."

" Yes," said the people round about, " the Honourable Mr Oguchi will know. He's one of the Christian people."

" How far is his house ? " said the country man. " My stupid knee will not let me travel far."

Then the rickshaw man said, " I know Mr Oguchi. Get up into my wheel chair and I will take you there."

" Are you a Christian, too, that you offer to help a stranger ? " asked a man standing near.

" Yes," said the rickshaw man with a friendly grin.

So the people in the crowd helped the man with the hurt knee to get into the rickshaw. The rickshaw man set off at a good trot and Taro and Haru ran beside. It was no use trying to find the foreign man now. Along the main road and down the narrow street they went till they came to Mr Oguchi's bookshop. The boys had just enough breath left to explain what had happened, while Mr Oguchi, smiling a welcome, helped the man out.

Mrs Oguchi set cushions on the floor for all the visitors, and while they gathered round the fire she hurried to bring them tea. As they sipped the hot drink the country man talked.

" I have worked in the city for many months, and O Haru San here rescued all the money that I have saved. Away among the mountains I have a daughter just as old as these boys here. O Tama San, my daughter, with her mother and grandmother have worked so hard while I have been away. Now I hope to be with them for the New Year, with money to buy seed for our fields."

But when the visitor tried to stand he was not so sure about the New Year, his knee was so stiff he could only walk when he leaned very heavily on Mr Oguchi's arm.

" It is far from my village, and there are many miles to walk from the nearest station," he said sadly.

Then Mr Oguchi had a plan. " I believe I can help," he said. " A friend of mine, a foreign man, goes near your village to-morrow in his car. It would not mean going many miles out of his way to take you home, and I'm sure he would be glad to give you a seat."

" How kind you are," said O Tama San's father, looking very puzzled. " But I'm a stranger ; why should you and your foreign friend help me like this ? "

" My friend is a follower of the Lord Jesus, and I seek to follow Him too. There are no ' strangers ' for us, but all are friends and brothers." Then he turned to Taro and Haru, who were listening hard. " Perhaps you would have time to wait while I write a letter and then take it to my foreign friend for me ? " he said, with a twinkle.

Taro smiled a very big smile as he said, " Why, of course we will ! " And he and Haru and the country man snuggled under the blanket round the warm stove while Mr Oguchi took his brush and ink stone and wrote his letter. As soon as he had finished it, he told the two boys where to find his friend's house, and off they ran into the snowy streets again. This time they did not knock anyone down on the way.

The very next morning they went to say good-bye to their country friend, and bowed to him as he set off for his home in the mountains. He looked so happy sitting in the front of the car, with Mr Oguchi's foreign friend sitting at the wheel and waving good-bye to them.

" Why not carve a motor-car, too, and put your foreign man inside," Haru suggested,

But Taro thought that would be too difficult.   Anyway he did know now just the shape of a foreign nose.

On New Year's morning there was a surprise present for Taro's father.   When he unwrapped the paper and looked at the gift Taro had made for him he said, " But this is exactly like a big foreign man.   Did you really carve him all by yourself ?   However did you find out just what he looked like ? "

And then Taro told his father all the story that we know.

     .   .   .   .   .   .

That same New Year's morning there was a very happy family in a little thatched house on the mountain-side. O Tama San thought she would never be tired of hearing of all her father's adventures in the big town.

" I should like to see the big city ! " said O Tama San.

Father looked sad.   " In the big city there is much to see, but there are few friends and many strangers."

" The bookshop man was kind to you," said mother.

" Yes, but he is not like others.   He told me he followed the Lord Jesus Christ, and that to the Christians none are strangers."

" What did he mean ? " asked O Baa San and mother and O Tama San, their eyes wide open with surprise.

" I asked the foreign man, and on the way home he told me a story more wonderful than any even O Baa San has ever heard or told."

" Tell us," they begged.

" He told how the great God who made the sun and the beautiful moon, all this lovely world and the people who live in it, loves all His children upon this earth.   He wanted everybody to know about His love and so He came to live on earth, and He was called Jesus.   He it is that Mr Oguchi follows. The Lord Jesus lived to show what the great God is like. He was the Friend of lonely strangers in big cities, of boys and girls in villages among the hills, of tired people who were weary with their work. He made sick people well and sad people glad. He loved the flowers as we do and taught that as God, the Heavenly Father, cares for them and makes them beautiful, so none of His children will ever lack anything they really need."

" Where is this Lord Jesus now ? " asked O Baa San.

" He had enemies who hated Him, but even these He went on loving, even these He would not treat as strangers. They killed Him but He lives again. Though we cannot see Him many know Him and follow Him, and grow like Him."

" May I thank Him for sending His friends to help you and for bringing you safely home, O Lo San ? " asked O Tama San.

" The Christians thank their God and I think we might all thank Him too." said father, " I'm sure He will understand what we say."

" I would like to hear more stories about Him," said O Tama San.

MISS FLOWER'S HOLIDAY

MISS FLOWER, a little girl of Burma, was really rather tired of listening to the rain music. Here was another day beginning, and as she lay on her mat she could hear the sound of it still—drip, drip, drip, drip ; from the feathery bamboo branches, from the big flapping leaves of the banana tree by the window, from the soft thatch of the little house where she and her grandmother lived. Drip ! Drip ! Splash ! That raindrop had come through the roof, right on Miss Flower's small nose ! It did that some-times. To-day she was tired of the rain. The river near the village had come tumbling over its banks two days ago and the brown flood-water was spreading over the paddy [1] fields ; even the path to school was partly under water. The country beside the river was so flat that the water came to all the hollow places and there it stayed. But, because everyone had come to school so regularly all through the rainy days, to-day was to be a half holiday, if the sun came out. Drip ! Drip ! Drip ! Perhaps the

[1] Young rice.

water had come under the house. Miss Flower turned over and put one eye close to a crack in the floor. The house where she lived was built on high posts, like stilts, just in case the floods spread over the garden. Only hens and pigs and chickens lived underneath on the ground floor. Miss Flower and grandmother, like all the other people in their village, live upstairs, and when you go to call on them you must climb a little ladder to the platform in front of the sleeping room.

This morning when Miss Flower peeped through the chink she saw that the ground was still dry. The chickens were huddled together, all fluffy feathered, keeping each other warm, but the old fat pig was already up and out, grunting and nosing round in the mud and looking hopefully for breakfast. Miss Flower remembered that she was hungry too. Grannie's mat was rolled up and put away in the corner, and Miss Flower could hear her moving about on the platform outside. She sat up, rolled up her own mat, and when she had said good-morning to her grandmother, ran down the ladder outside. Under the house stood a big earthenware jar full of water, so under the house was the place where you tubbed, and Miss Flower gave herself an extra special cleaning because to-day might be a holiday. Teeth cleaning was a very thorough business, too, with a tooth powder made of charcoal and salt and fingers for a toothbrush. Miss Flower was up the ladder again in a very short time, rooting among her treasures that lived in a small red box in the sleeping room. Out came one small piece of broken mirror, without a frame, a flat smooth stone and a strip of tree bark. A cup of water was standing near, and Miss Flower was soon very busy, first damping the bark and then rubbing it on the stone, making a thick flowery-looking paste. She was so quiet that grannie peeped in and watched her, smiled and went away again. Miss Flower's " beauty stone " was one of her greatest treasures. Now she was squatting on her heels, the mirror propped on the box, covering her honey-coloured face with the paste, as she had seen the big girls do. Next she combed her straight jet-black hair. It was not very long yet. If she bent her head right back, she could just reach the end and pull it. When she was big she meant to have a shining coil right on the top of her head. Now she was seven years old it really was time to start that coil. All the hair that would meet at the top she gathered together and bound tightly round with bright pink thread, so that the hair ends stuck out like a stiff little paintbrush.

"Grannie, grannie," she called. "Do come and see; I have a real hair-knot on my head. It will soon be as big as yours."

Grannie came to the doorway again and nodded and smiled. " So it will, so it will. We must pick a flower to pin to your hair-knot, when the rain stops. But the food is ready now, come and eat."

Miss Flower very soon finished dressing. She wrapped her long red and white skirt very tightly round and fixed it in a firm fold in front. Then she put on a dainty white blouse. One hand went up to feel if the hair-knot was still there, and then she walked quite slowly out to breakfast, because she felt so big.

Grannie had spread a mat on the platform outside the sleeping room. Plates on which steaming rice was heaped in great white mountains, and little bowls of curry, stood ready on a small low table. There was a roof, made of strong new bamboo matting, over the half of the platform where they sat for breakfast, and that was a good thing. As it was, it was rather wet and drippy, for the rain came driving through the open sides.

Grannie bent her head and closed her eyes. " We will

say ' Thank you ' to our Heavenly Father for breakfast and for rain that makes the paddy grow."

Miss Flower *was* thankful for breakfast, but she wasn't so sure about the rain, so she just said, " Thank you for the food we eat," and added another little prayer of her own, " and if there is enough rain for the paddy now, please may we have a fine day ? "

" If it stops raining," said grannie, who had not heard Miss Flower's own special prayer, " we will go fishing this afternoon."

" Drip ! Drip ! Drip ! " laughed the raindrops, but Miss Flower was quite sure the sky was not so dark.

She and grannie were soon busy making the rice mountains disappear. First they took a little helping of the

white grains, with the tips of the fingers of the right hand. It would be very bad manners to take food with the left hand, and Miss Flower had been taught that just as soon as she was old enough to remember which was left and which was right. Then the rice was dipped into a curry bowl, and that turned it a lovely golden colour. With a quick, clever twist of her fingers Miss Flower made a ball of the rice, and then with a flick of her thumb that golden ball shot into her mouth.

When fingers were washed and the plates and bowls put away, grannie went into the sleeping room and brought out a huge hat made of bamboo, as big as an umbrella, and put it on Miss Flower's head. "That will keep you dry," she said. "Go carefully where the flood-water is across the path."

Miss Flower promised and then climbed down the ladder. Grannie sat on the top step and watched her go. "Good-bye, little mushroom," she called.

There were other moving "mushrooms" to be seen by this time, as the boys and girls, all wearing the big umbrella hats, came splashing along the pathways that led from homes to school.

Miss Flower ran up the school ladder and took off her big mushroom hat the very minute she was under the thatch and in the dry. Her two friends, Miss Goat and Miss Coconut, were there before her.

"Look at my hair-knot," she said, bending down to show them her stiff little tuft. "Grandmother says it is big enough to wear a flower. I'm going to pick one, when the rain stops."

" Drip ! Drip ! Drip ! " sang the rain, but much more slowly now, as if it was feeling tired. Now the boys were coming—Master Green and Black Egg, Small Fish and Light and White King. They sat on the floor on one side of the room and Miss Flower and the other girls sat on the other side. First came prayers, then lessons. Suddenly Miss Flower looked up, a sunbeam was resting on a yellow creeper that grew over the school fence, making it shine like gold. "The rain has stopped!" cried Miss Flower. "Shall we have a holiday ? "

" Who said holidays ? " called a voice from the garden.

" It's Thra," whispered the boys and girls : all eyes now turned towards the top of the ladder. First they saw a head of fair hair, then blue eyes smiling at them through a pair of glasses, then broad shoulders, and very soon the whole tall missionary was standing under the low thatch of their schoolroom. For this was a missionary school, where the Burmese boys and girls were being taught.

" We have not had much time for playing out of doors since the rain came, have we ? And you have all turned up at school in spite of all the wetness," he said. " I think we *will* have a holiday. What will you do, Black Egg ? "

" I shall mind the buffaloes, down by the flood."

" We're going to the bridge to catch the branches that come floating down and pull them out for firewood."

" My father will start to plough his fields," said White King, " and I shall help."

" Be sure you drive the bullocks straight. What will you do, Miss Goat ? "

" My mother is going to the market to buy a new yellow and red umbrella."

" I'm going fishing with my grandmother," said Miss Flower, who thought her plan was best of all.

" Look out for me," said Thra, " I'm going to the village across the flood-water in my dug-out canoe. Shall I tell the fishes to keep out of your way ? "

It was not easy to remember lessons for the rest of the morning, and at last it was time to go home and start holidays.

Grannie was sitting on the top step of the ladder again, when Miss Flower came running back from school. By her side was a deep basket that she had just finished weaving, with strips of split bamboo. She had plaited the border into a beautiful pattern and the basket was nearly deep enough for Miss Flower herself to get inside.

"What a lovely basket, grannie. Do you think we shall *fill* it with fish this afternoon ? "

"Plenty of water means plenty of fish. We shall see," said grannie.

Miss Flower was in such a hurry to be off she could scarcely wait while grandmother found the nets, a big one and a little one, each fixed to a bamboo pole. At last they both climbed down the ladder and set off for the fishing place. Miss Flower stopped to pick two sprays of white jasmine flowers that had opened to greet the sunshine, and pinned one in her grandmother's grey hair and one in her own black tuft. She and grannie both needed to walk carefully along the paths to keep their pretty skirts out of the mud. Miss Flower carried the nets and grandmother the big new fish basket. A gay coloured bag was slung on Miss Flower's shoulder too, for their way lay through the market and there was shopping to be done and there would be parcels to carry.

Grandmother bought a length of pink silk for a new Sunday skirt, and the tailor joined the side seam with his sewing-machine.

"There you are," he said, as he handed grandmother her skirt, now made and ready to wear. "That will be another one and a half annas."

So that was the first parcel for Miss Flower to carry in her bag. Next they stopped in front of a woman who was sitting under the shade of an umbrella as big as a tent, and beside her, on the ground, was a huge basket filled with bundles of tobacco leaves. Grannie loved to puff away at a big cheroot, so she bought new tobacco leaves to make a fresh supply of smokes. Now Miss Flower had two parcels in her bag.

One more stall had to be visited, at least Miss Flower

thought so, and always found the shortest cut through the market was by the woman who sold sugar cane. When the usual bargain game was over Miss Flower went along happily with a foot and a half of juicy red sugar cane to chew. That third parcel did not go into the bag !

Shopping over, the two went on towards the fishing place. The flooded river had spread water over many fields on both sides of its usual bed. What a wide stretch it was ! Now that the sun was shining the flood water did not look brown and dirty, but shimmered and danced in the light. Miss Flower put the deep basket on a sandy hillock near the water's edge, under the cool shade of a clump of bamboos. Then she and grannie squatted on their heels and watched for fishes. Perhaps it did not matter very much that most of the fishes wanted to swim the other way. The little breeze that made waves on the water was cool, and there were so many things to watch.

Four fishermen had beached their canoes on the edge of the flooded river nearby and were stretching a net over a cradle-shaped frame made of bamboo. Now they were letting it down from a bank where the waters were flowing swiftly. Any fishes swimming that way would *have* to swim into their net. Up it came again with a silver load. Far away, where the big river flowed, Miss Flower could see what looked like a little floating village. When she shaded her eyes she could see the thatched roofs of two houses and the red and yellow and pinks of women's skirts and men's bright head scarfs. That was a raft of teak logs on its long journey from the forest country to the sea, carrying not only the people who steered it, but their homes as well. How quickly it was moving, now that the river was in flood !

Black Egg had brought his father's buffaloes to wallow in the water. The first of them had waded in so far that all of him except his black nose was hidden. Another had not waded quite so far, and two snow-white **paddy birds** were perched on the ridge of his shiny black back. Like Miss Flower they were watching for fishes. A tiny scarlet bird skimmed over the water and Miss Flower watched it until it was a speck. Then she saw something else, much bigger, moving nearer to their fishing place.

"Look, grannie," she said, pointing over the water, "there's Thra. He said he was going over the flood in his own canoe."

"It's not a very good canoe," said grannie. "See how low it is in the water."

Thra's boat was a hollow tree trunk, thick and heavy and clumsy. He had only a stick for a paddle, but he did seem to be coming nearer, moving along somehow. His open umbrella was fixed where it caught the wind like a sail.

Miss Flower stood up to wave to him. "Please tell the fishes to come this way ! " she shouted.

Grannie chuckled. "Mind he doesn't go to the bottom to give them your message!" She went on skimming her net over the water nearby, not watching Thra. Thra did not seem to hear Miss Flower; he was looking down into his boat. He was so big and top-heavy, and now only the tiniest rim of boat showed above the surface of the water. Then suddenly down went the tree canoe, right under the water, and there was big Thra spluttering in the dirty flood, his hat floating one way, his umbrella, upside down, sailing merrily towards grannie and Miss Flower.

Miss Flower shouted as loud as ever she could, "Grannie! Grannie! Thra's in the water!"

Grannie did look then, and she stood up and shouted too. Black Egg heard and joined the chorus. "Thra's in the water! Thra's boat has sunk!" Some other fishermen nearby heard and were soon busy launching their own canoes to go to Thra's help. Thra managed to swim to a post that was sticking out of the flood, but his clothes were so heavy with muddy water that he could not get any farther.

At last the men reached him and helped him to the sandy bank where Miss Flower was waiting with the umbrella she had saved. "Oh, Thra, did you go to the bottom to give the fishes my message?"

Thra laughed. "I told you I would tell them Miss Flower was going fishing, and now you've caught me instead!"

"Come to see us this evening," said grannie, "and we will show you what else we've caught. It was a good thing that Miss Flower saw you just now."

"Indeed it was, and now I'm going home to get dry," said Thra.

That evening Miss Flower and grannie were sitting on their own special steps on the ladder, grannie on the top step and Miss Flower on the bottom rung but one. They had

just finished a lovely supper of rice and curried fish and
grannie was making cheroots. She had chopped the new
tobacco leaves with her cooking knife and was filling the
sheaths of maize cob leaves that Miss Flower was handing
up to her. Only grannie's practised fingers could roll the
cheroot tightly enough when once the sheaths were filled.

"Do you think Thra will really come?" said Miss Flower.
"I've picked such a lovely cucumber for him."

"Yes, here he is," said grannie.

And into the garden came Thra, dry again now. Grannie
shook her head at him. "Please don't try to travel in a
dug-out canoe again," she said.

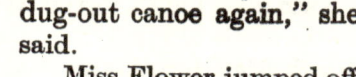

Miss Flower jumped off
her step and ran up into
the house. Soon she came
back with a little string
of fishes and a big green
cucumber. "These are for
you," she said, handing
them to Thra.

Thra smiled and said
thank you once again.

"Now who is coming to
school for evening prayers? We are going to give thanks
together to our Heavenly Father for rain for the paddy
fields, for sunshine and a holiday, and for the sharp eyes
of a little girl with a hair-knot on her head who helped to
rescue a very wet missionary."

So grannie climbed down the ladder, and Miss Flower too,
and they both went with Thra to give thanks.